Jeremiah th
and the Day of Palms

An Adventure to Jerusalem

By Pastor Danny R. Hammons

Illustrations by Robin T. Nelson

Colibri Children's Press
An imprint of Colibri Children's Adventures
Gales Ferry, CT

Colibri Children's Press
An imprint of Colibri Children's Adventures
16 Inchcliffe Drive
Gales Ferry, CT 06335
www.ColibriChildrensPress.com

ISBN 978-0-9998744-0-0 hard cover
ISBN 978-0-9998744-1-7 soft cover
ISBN 978-0-9998744-2-4 ebook

Publisher's Cataloging-In-Publication Data
(Prepared by The Donohue Group, Inc.)

Names: Hammons, Danny. | Nelson, Robin T., illustrator.
Title: Jeremiah the donkey and the Day of Palms : an adventure to
   Jerusalem / by Pastor Danny Hammons ; illustrations by Robin T. Nelson.
Description: Gales Ferry, CT : Colibri Children's Adventures LLC, [2018] |
   Interest age level: 004-010. | Summary: "This whimsical tale offers a
   unique perspective about Palm Sunday from the viewpoint of a young
   donkey colt, Jeremiah. It gives children the realization that even
   though we'd all like to just play and jump around, there are times when
   each of us is called to perform a special task, which can be just as
   rewarding. Questions for discussion with children and fun facts about
   donkeys as they were used in biblical times are included."--Provided by
   publisher.
Identifiers: ISBN 9780999874400 (hardcover) | ISBN 9780999874417
   (softcover) | ISBN 9780999874424 (ebook)
Subjects: LCSH: Donkeys--Juvenile fiction. | Duty--Juvenile fiction. |
   Palm Sunday--Juvenile fiction. | CYAC: Donkeys--Fiction. | Duty--
   Fiction. | Palm Sunday--Fiction. | GSAFD: Christian fiction.
Classification: LCC PZ7.1.H3633 Je 2018 (print) | LCC PZ7.1.H3633 (ebook)
   | DDC [E]--dc23

Printed in the United States of America

Dedication

To my parents,
Kathryn Callahan Hammons and **Daniel Thomas Hammons**,
who were always there for me, and helped me to grow in faith.
They taught me about God's love and were my first models of what
it meant to live a faithful life. I miss them both very much.

Acknowledgments

Sunday School teachers – especially those who taught me, and
those at St. Luke, Gales Ferry and St. John's, Parkville – thank you
for your devotion to helping our children and youth learn about
God's unconditional love!

Robin T. Nelson – Thank you for making my story come alive with
your wonderful illustrations. This wouldn't have happened without
your willingness to share your gifts.

Maria Janow Hammons – Thank you, my most precious wife, for
your love and support, and for encouraging me to put my stories
down on paper. I love you so very much!

Jeremiah the Donkey was out playing in the field one day, kicking at some rocks.

1

All Jeremiah really wanted to do was to continue playing, kicking the rocks and bushes.

All of a sudden, he saw the man who owned him coming toward him with a rope.

"What's this guy going to do?" Jeremiah asked himself.

His owner led him next to his mother and tied him to a post.

Jeremiah," his mother said in a voice that always calmed him. "You are going on a great adventure like your grandmother once did. She carried a woman who was going to have a baby on a long journey and it was amazing. I'll tell you about it when you come home from your adventure."

4

Jeremiah watched as his owner walked over to two men whom Jeremiah had never seen before. They talked for a while and shook hands.

Jeremiah could not understand people talk.
He just listened to the sounds of their voices.

Blah....blah!

Blah ...... blah .... blah..

The men untied Jeremiah and led him out of the village.

All Jeremiah could hear was the sound of all the people making these silly noises.

"Blah...Blah, Blah, Blah!"

Jeremiah shook his head and let out a loud

"HEE HAW, HEE HAW"

Everyone jumped off the road as Jeremiah walked by.

Jeremiah was smiling all the way, as people jumped and moved out of his way every time he cried:

"HEE HAW, HEE HAW"

This is fun Jeremiah thought.

They went down the hillside from the village, across the valley, and up the Mount of Olives, all the way to a place called Bethany.

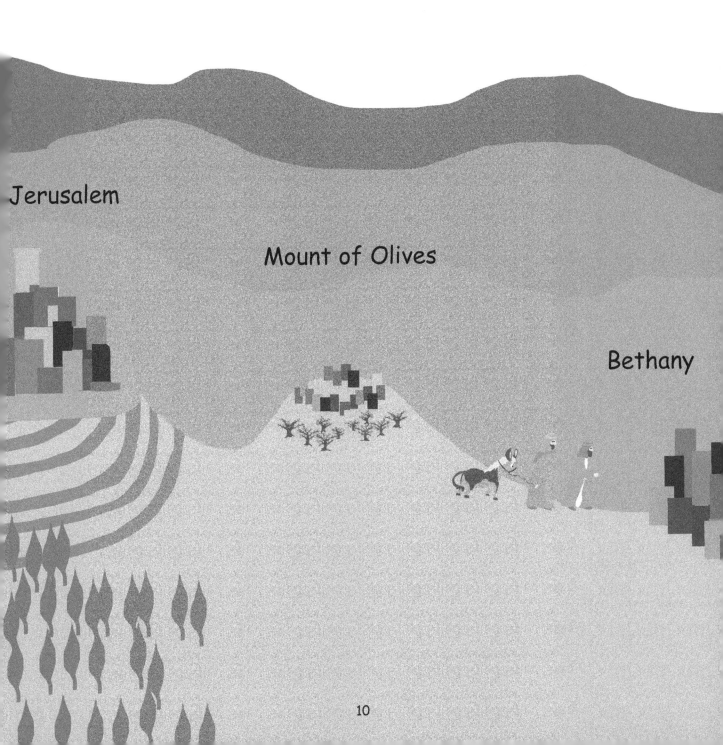

Jerusalem

Mount of Olives

Bethany

When they got to Bethany, Jeremiah saw another man standing with ten other men and they were making those silly noises again.

11

Just then, the man turned around and smiled at Jeremiah.

Jeremiah saw that this man had a very kind face. He was different from any other man that he had seen during his short life.

The two men, who led Jeremiah to this kind man, put a blanket on Jeremiah's back.

Then the man with the very kind face sat down on Jeremiah.

"What's this," he thought? "No one has ever done this to me before. What am I supposed to do? Maybe I could start kicking."

"No," Jeremiah thought. "This man is kind and gentle. What do you think he wants me to do?"

As this kind man gently petted Jeremiah's head, he decided to calmly start back down the same road.

This time things were different as he walked down the hill and across the valley carrying this very kind man on his back.

Not once did he cry out.

This time when the people saw the kind man and Jeremiah, they moved out of the way. They were not afraid.

This made Jeremiah feel very proud.
Now he strutted all the way down the hill.

He looked to the right and to the left at all the people getting out of their way and Jeremiah smiled.

Jeremiah saw the gates of the city.
They were as tall as the sky.

All the people began to make their silly noises together.
Jeremiah was not afraid as they sang their song.

"Blah...blah Blah Blah Blah"

Then the kind man touched Jeremiah's ears. All of a sudden, the silly noises began to make sense to Jeremiah.

He no longer heard:

"Blah...blah Blah Blah Blah"

Now he understood them. They were singing.

"Hosanna to the Son of David!
Blessed is the one who comes in the name of the Lord!
Hosanna in the highest heaven!"

Hosanna to the Son of David!

Jeremiah lifted his head and strutted proudly carrying the King into the city.

Then they bowed down to the ground and laid their coats and palm branches on the ground for the King and Jeremiah to walk on.

Everyone continued to sing out.

"Hosanna! Hosanna!"

All the way to a house in the city.

Hosanna, Hosanna, Hosanna!

Hosanna, Hosanna, Hosanna!

When they were in front of the house, the kind man asked Jeremiah to stop....and he did.

The kind man got off Jeremiah and stood in front of him.

He smiled at Jeremiah and said, "Thank you, Jeremiah for the ride. My name is Jesus."

Then Jesus rubbed Jeremiah's head and went into the building with the other men.

Jeremiah was so happy. Wow! This is
the best day of my life.

"HEE HAW, HEE HAW, HEE HAW!!!"

Jeremiah thought to himself, "The people will always remember this day as the

Day of Palms."

They were all so happy to see King Jesus and lay down their palms in front of him.

This kind man was Jesus the King, the Son of David, and he, Jeremiah the Donkey, had carried the King into Jerusalem on his back.

Wow!
What a day!

Questions after you have read the book.

1. Jesus rode on a donkey. What other story in the Bible features a donkey?
2. Jeremiah's owner talks to two men at the beginning of the book. These two men lead Jeremiah to Jesus where he is talking to ten more men. Who could these twelve men be?
3. When the people heard that Jesus was coming into Jerusalem what did they do?
4. When people saw Jesus, what did they call Him?
5. In the story, the people shouted Hosanna. Do you know what this means?
6. What did the people put on the ground? Why did they do this?
7. How was Jeremiah different after he met Jesus?

Fun facts about donkeys in Jesus' time.

1. Did you know that donkeys were used by all kinds of people to travel from place to place? The saddles they used were simple, made of cloth or animal skins.

2. Both women and men rode donkeys. But if a woman was riding there was always a driver, that is someone who walked beside the donkey and led it along the way. Do you remember the story of Mary riding the donkey into Bethlehem when Joseph walked?

3. Riding a donkey was a sign of peace. Horses were used during war.

4. Donkeys were used for other things too. They were used to carry the fruit, grain, and vegetables from the farms to the market. Sometimes they were used to plough fields to plant the grain and sometimes for pulling the big wheel that ground the grain into flour.

Check the website for more
Activities, Coloring Sheets, and Fun Facts
www.ColibriChildrensPress.com

Author

The **Reverend Danny R. Hammons** received his Master of Divinity and a Master of Sacred Theology from the Lutheran Theological Seminary at Gettysburg. He also holds a Bachelor of Arts in History and Language from the University of Maryland. Pastor Danny serves as the Lead Pastor of St. Luke Lutheran Church in Gales Ferry, Connecticut. He previously served as co-pastor with his wife, the Reverend Maria J. Hammons, at St. John's Lutheran Church in Baltimore, Maryland.

One of Pastor Danny's greatest joys is teaching children (of all ages) about God's love, especially sharing God's story during Sunday morning children's sermon time. You can often find Pastor Danny carrying out his ministry with his rescue pal Riley - his best buddy and constant canine companion.

Illustrator

Robin T. Nelson is a children's book writer and illustrator who has studied watercolor painting at the Lyme Academy of Fine Art. She follows the color theory of the artist Stephen Quiller, with whom she has taken several workshops. She recently retired from many years as a research scientist and can now devote more time to art. Robin is a scientist at heart, a devoted wife and mother, and enjoys using her artistic skills for humanitarian purposes.

CPSIA information can be obtained
at www.ICGtesting.com
Printed in the USA
BVHW02s1156010418
511892BV00017BA/258/P